The Busy
Little Squirrel

The Busy Little Squirrel

Nancy Tafuri

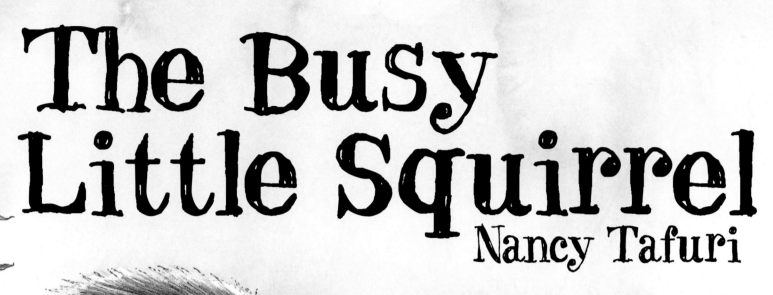

Simon & Schuster Books for Young Readers
New York   London   Toronto   Sydney

Leaves were falling.
The air was getting cold.

It was time for Squirrel
to get ready for winter.

"Squeak, squeak," said Mouse.
"Will you nibble a pumpkin with us?"

But Squirrel couldn't . . .

He was so busy!

"Sweet, sweet," said Bird.
"Will you rest on a branch with us?"

But Squirrel couldn't . . .

He was so busy!

"Croak, croak," said Frog.
"Will you hop rocks with us?"

But Squirrel couldn't . . .

He was so busy!

He was so busy!

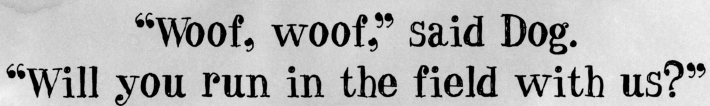

"Woof, woof," said Dog.
"Will you run in the field with us?"

But Squirrel couldn't . . .

He was so busy!

"Hoo-hoo, hoo-hoo," called Owl.
"Will you watch the moon with us?"

But Squirrel couldn't . . .

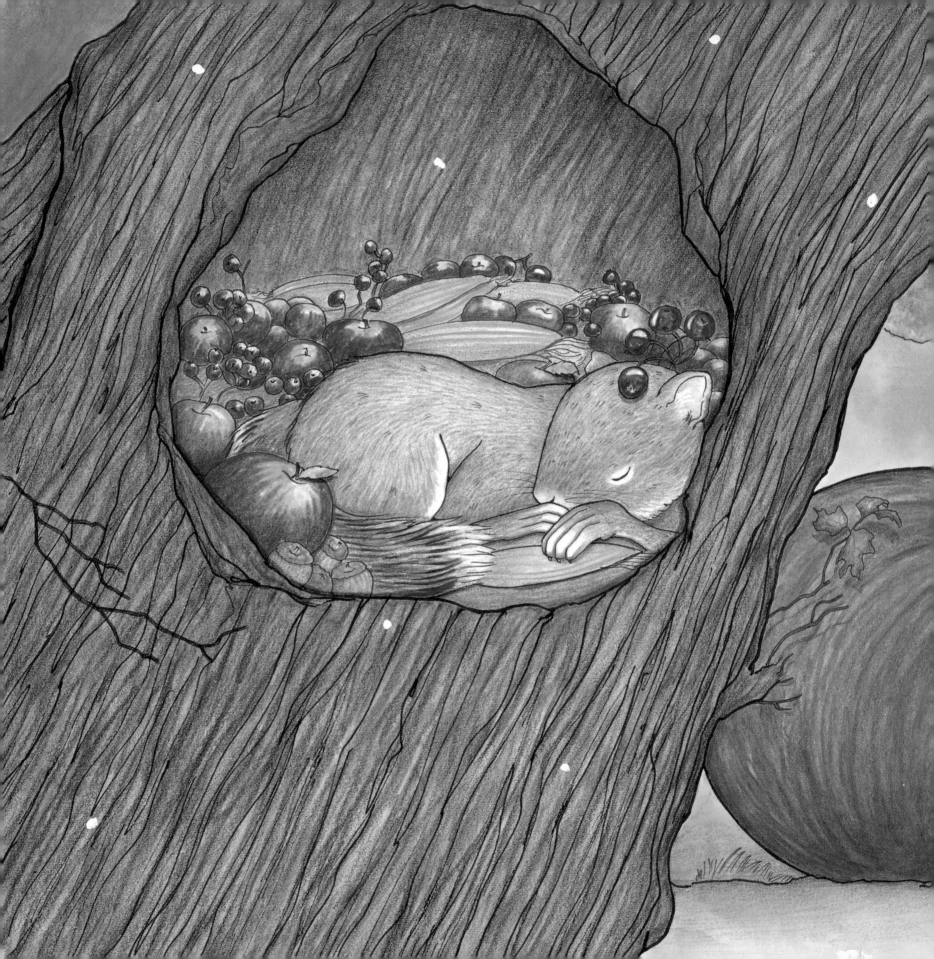

He was fast asleep!

FOR MARY–my very busy friend

SIMON & SCHUSTER BOOKS FOR YOUNG READERS · An imprint of Simon & Schuster Children's Publishing Division · 1230 Avenue of the Americas, New York, New York 10020 · Copyright © 2007 by Nancy Tafuri · All rights reserved, including the right of reproduction in whole or in part in any form. · SIMON & SCHUSTER BOOKS FOR YOUNG READERS is a trademark of Simon & Schuster, Inc. · Book design by Lucy Ruth Cummins · The text for this book is set in Blue Century. · The illustrations for this book are rendered in brush pen, watercolor pencils, and ink. · Manufactured in China ·   10 9 8 7 6 5 4   · Library of Congress Cataloging-in-Publication Data · Tafuri, Nancy. · The busy little squirrel / Nancy Tafuri.—1st ed. · p. cm. · Summary: Squirrel is too busy getting ready for winter to nibble a pumpkin with Mouse, run in the field with Dog, or otherwise play with any of the other animals. · ISBN-13: 978-0-689-87341-6 · ISBN-10: 0-689-87341-7 · [1. Squirrels—Fiction. 2. Animals—Fiction.] I. Title. · PZ7.T117Om 2006 · [Fic]—dc 22 · 2005015520